MOONSTONE MURDERS

The Movie Script

by

WILLIAM MALTESE

The Borgo Press
An Imprint of Wildside Press

MMVII

FIRST EDITION

MOONSTONE MURDERS

CONTENTS

Introduction 7

Moonstone Murders 9

About the Author................................... 135

INTRODUCTION

This book comes to you for several reasons.

Firstly, my agent requested that I do an m/m movie script so that he could "shop" it around; more specifically, the runaway success of *Brokeback Mountain* had suddenly put "gay" movies in vogue. He had also received feelers from a producer of mainly gay porn who was looking to upgrade his company and his products' image by possibly putting into production something a little more mainstream and less in-your-face (pun intended) than his usual fare.

Shortly after I'd completed the script and passed it onto my agent, and my agent had sent it to the production company, my agent passed away. By the time the producer got back to me with his request to "possibly work with him" in getting the script "just right," I'd lost interest, having already moved on to other things.

Secondly, I recently came across the script in a drawer and, reading it over after having not seen it for awhile, I realized how the format made it far easier and faster to read than a standard novel. I had this confirmed by handing it over to a friend of mine who exhibits all of the typical tendencies of the "today" generation: he has a rather short attention span, he would rather play a computer game than read a book, and if and when he does read anything, besides game instructions, it tends to be comic books.

Therefore, I figured the script format might be a way to attract new readers (what author doesn't want new readers?); the publication of a script usually only happens "in-house" at the studio where the movie is being made, and it is seldom made available to the general public.

Thirdly (last but not least), I put my idea to my editor at the Borgo Press imprint of Wildside Press, with whom I presently have an excellent working relationship, and he said, "Sure, why not give it a try?"

So—drum roll, please—here's the result, which, I hope, may persuade someone who thinks books are too long, too boring, or too time-consuming, to take a chance on *Moonstone Murders* (even without the attending pictures). Who knows: you may even like it!

—William Maltese
May 2007

MOONSTONE MURDERS

FADE IN:

PARIS, FRANCE
INT TOWN HOUSE

LANDON JORDAN AT 14 reads a letter from his father as

CLARK MOIRE, 14, joins him.

CLARK
Something from your father? More scrimshaw?

Clark looks at the two small stones from Landon's father that Landon shows him.

CLARK
Oh. Not more scrimshaw.

LANDON AT 14
Impressed?

CLARK
Rocks. Two.

Landon holds one small stone to his ear.

LANDON AT 14
Earring?

Landon moves the stone to the middle of his chest.

LANDON AT 14
Necklace?

CLARK
Your father must know you have all the rocks you need—in your head.

LANDON AT 14
So much for testing your knowledge of astronomy.

CLARK
Don't you mean geology?

LANDON AT 14
You don't know meteorites when you see them.

CLARK
What meteorites?

LANDON AT 14
These. Pieces anyway. From the two large ones that fell within two nights of each other on some wilderness property we own in Canada.

CLARK
You're lying.

LANDON AT 14
Am not.
(reads from his father's letter)
"I sold the two meteorites to a Mr. Kyle Wynard who's going to use the metal to make art knives. He commissioned me to do the scrimshaw hilts. But knowing how fond of those meteorites you are, I saved you these bits as souvenirs."

CLARK
You made it up.
(takes letter from Landon)
You actually saw two meteorites come down?

LANDON AT 14
Not me. My parents weren't even married at the time. Dad saw them. Almost fried to a crisp in the fire set by one of them. There they still were, though, poking out of the ground every summer we went to the mountains.

CLARK
Neat.

LANDON AT 14
I'd pretend they were spaceships that could take me to the moon.

CLARK
No.

LANDON AT 14
I was younger, then. Wanted to be an astronaut.

CLARK
When did you ever want to be an astronaut.

LANDON AT 14
Right after I decided I didn't want to be a policeman.

MRS. MOIRE calls from elsewhere in the house.

MRS. MOIRE
Clark, are you and Landon coming?

CLARK
(to Landon)
Bring your rocks and turn smarty Marty peagreen with envy.

CUT TO:

BAGHDAD, IRAQ (DURING THE WAR)

INT U.S. ARMY HEADQUARTERS

COLONEL ROBERT KENTETH sits at his desk. LIEUTENANT JAKE DENNISON stands before him.

ROBERT
Such fuss over a knife.

JAKE

Religious significance. Some prophet of import dropped it out of the sky for some imam in some jihad—or something like that.

ROBERT

What makes them think it was snatched by one of ours?

JAKE

He was in uniform.

ROBERT

Right. He could have done himself one better by sticking a flashing red light on his forehead. Anyone else see this as a set-up?

JAKE

Not much thinking, period. Emotions high. A witness swears he's seen the officer before. Around. In a bar. On the street. Outside the museum. Nothing specific, by way of description, though—except dark hair.

ROBERT

Rank, uniform, and hair color. Great!

JAKE

All we Christians look alike to Moslems. But the guy swears he'll know him again when he sees him.

ROBERT
I'll bet. Keep me posted, preferably sooner than later.
(Jake leaves. Robert picks up the phone)
(over phone)
Silner, get in here!

CUT TO:

INT BUILDING/OUTSKIRTS BAGHDAD

Robert knocks on the door.

ROBERT
(calling through door)
Silner told me you're here.

MAN IN SKI MASK *opens the door.*

ROBERT
Had to take it, didn't you?

Robert pushes inside.

ROBERT
You were spotted, did you know that? Wore your uniform. What a jackass thing to do. Your little green spacemen buddies tell you they'd wrapped you in an invisible cloak, did they? If so, it didn't work and, as usual, your mess is mine to clean up. Take off that stupid mask!

Man in Ski Mask turns his back on Robert and walks to a door which opens into another room; he steps through the door and closes it behind him.

ROBERT
(calling after)
You're a certifiable nut-case. Those hustlers: bad enough, but what's a few dead queers? This? You'll be lucky if I can save your ass. You're out of here as soon as your orders can be cut. Hear me? I don't want to know how good business is doing.

INT OTHER ROOM
P.O.V.—MAN IN SKI MASK

*Man in Ski Mask carefully unrolls a silk wrapper to reveal the knife within. He picks up the knife. On the bed, an **IRAQI HUSTLER** is naked, tied and gagged.*

ROBERT
(from other room)
No way does that knife leave here. You have other knives, you crazy bastard, and there'll be hell to pay if this one isn't returned. Got that?

The Man in Ski Mask goes to the Iraqi Hustler. With the tip of the knife, he begins to cut a bloody line diagonally across the guy's chest. The Iraqi hustler screams.

CUT TO:

EXT DUSTY ROAD OUTSIDE BAGHDAD

The Iraqi Hustler, knife striations all over his naked body, lies dead by the side of the road.

EXT U.S. ARMY HEADQUARTERS

EXT MILITARY AREA / BAGHDAD AIRPORT

A military transport plane takes off for the U.S.

CUT TO:

PACIFIC NORTHWEST, U.S.

EXT WYNARD COUNTRY ESTATE/HOUSE
NIGHT

INT WYNARD COUNTRY ESTATE/DEN

Man in Ski Mask steals a collection of one-hundred-sixty art knives. He puts majority in small suitcase. He separates three knives, two of which have scrimshaw handles, and puts them in a special sponge-lined briefcase. The suitcase, when shut, springs its latch. Man in Ski Mask puts suitcase under his arm to keep it shut as he prepares to leave with it and the briefcase.

INT WYNARD COUNTRY ESTATE/MAIN-HOUSE ENTRANCE
NIGHT

*Man in Ski Mask comes down stairs. **KYLE WYNARD** enters through front door. Struggle occurs.*

16

Contents of suitcase spill. Man in Ski Mask accesses one of the scattered knives and kills Kyle.

CUT TO:

TEN YEARS LATER

PACIFIC NORTHWEST, U.S.

INT U.S. ARMY HELICOPTER/CARGO BAY

THREE MEN *fasten down a meteorite.*

EXT WOODED AREA/METEORITE RECOVERY SITE FOGGY/RAINY DAY

The Three Men exit helicopter and walk passed ***STEVE HOWARD*** *and the* ***HELICOPTER PILOT***.

PILOT
(to Steve)
   It's leave now, or get socked in.

STEVE
   I'll get Landon.

Steve enters nearby pitched tent.

INT.TENT

LANDON JORDAN *throws personal things in a knapsack.*

17

STEVE
Ready?

LANDON
Yes.

STEVE
Thanks again. Without your help, Christian Wynard would have beaten us here for sure.

LANDON
Glad to help. Even if it has been awhile since Dad turned all of this over to the park system. Ages since I've been here. Then, this wretched weather.

STEVE
Another meteorite for science, saved from conversion into yet another unnecessary knife blade. Score one for us good guys.

Steve and Landon exit the tent.

EXT TENT

CHRISTIAN WYNARD *joins Steve and Landon.*

CHRISTIAN
I need a lift. Can you oblige?

STEVE
People in hell need ice water.

CHRISTIAN
Be nice. You did win.

STEVE
Not through any help from you.

CHRISTIAN
I'm a generous loser. Are you a generous winner?

STEVE
Where's your own chopper?

CHRISTIAN
I hiked in, remember? Mine can't possibly get here before I'm socked in.

STEVE
Okay, why not? If Landon can stand your company, that is.

LANDON
I think I can manage it as far as Vancouver.

Landon and Christian brave the downdraft from the helicopter and enter the cargo bay; Steve stays behind.

INT U.S. ARMY HELICOPTER/CARGO BAY

Landon and Christian strap themselves into seats.

CHRISTIAN
Does Steve really see me as a monster personified?

LANDON
As an Alberich complete with smoking forge.

CHRISTIAN
That how you see me, too? That why you didn't help the son of the man who made knives with your father?

LANDON
Your father made knives. My father made hilts. Besides, you didn't ask for my help. Steve did, to the supposed benefit of U.S.-subsidized cosmic research.

The helicopter takes off.

CUT TO:

EXT U.S. ARMY HELICOPTER/
ABOVE CLOUD COVER

SOUND of TWO MUFFLED but almost simultaneous EXPLOSIONS. The U.S. Army Helicopter stalls, goes down, hits mid-river, and washes toward the lip of a waterfall.

INT U.S. ARMY HELICOPTER/CARGO BAY
P.O.V.—LANDON

Cables holding the meteorite SNAP.

20

CUT TO:

EXT GORGE/DOWNRIVER FROM WATER-FALL FOGGY/RAINY DAY

Landon, half in and half out of the river, tries to beach himself but fails. A drenched Christian, already on shore, arrives and gives a helping hand. Christian tries to help Landon walk, the latter finally out of the water. Landon can't manage.

LANDON
Sorry.

Landon passes out. Christian picks him up and carries him.

CUT TO:

INT CAVE

Landon regains consciousness. Christian attends a fire.

CHRISTIAN
I have good news and bad.

LANDON
Where are we?

CHRISTIAN
In a cave with plenty of dry wood. That's the good news. The bad news: it's driftwood that got

here by riding the river. Question: When is the next batch due?

LANDON
How'd you manage the fire? Two-sticks together and all that? Color me impressed.

CHRISTIAN
Fire compliments of dear dad.

LANDON
His ghost, you mean?

Christian produces a knife from one boot.

CHRISTIAN
One of his hand-crafted survival knives. The hollow handle contains a compass, wire saw, waterproof matches. Everything, except food, needed by any man, or men, stranded in the middle of nowhere. I bought it last month from its original buyer, a hunter in Idaho who swore by it for the twenty-five years he owned it.

LANDON
I take back everything derogatory I ever said about knives.

CHRISTIAN
Said a few derogatory things about knives, have you?

LANDON

There was this paring knife that cut me to the bone. There was this Boy Scout knife owned by Jerry Salinas. Come to think of it, some of the derogatory things said, in that case, were probably about Jerry.

CHRISTIAN

Our fathers made a good team, but you never experimented along similar lines, did you? Not that, with several successful art galleries, you seem to have suffered from the oversight.

LANDON

I've an interesting observation of my own.

CHRISTIAN

Couldn't be how I got turned on to knives despite my father having been killed by one?

LANDON

None of my business. Credit my deteriorated condition. I can't get warm.

CHRISTIAN

We should be out of these wet clothes.

LANDON

Right. More gooseflesh likely to keep us so much warmer.

CHRISTIAN

There's always heat-generating sex.

LANDON
You hold your breath, and I'll tell you when.

CHRISTIAN
Everything else considered, you okay?

LANDON
I've not the foggiest notion of anything after the chopper hit ground, water, whatever, and my waking up here. Unless you're twins, I'm seeing double. You?

CHRISTIAN
In one piece, as far as I can tell.

There are SOUNDS like COLLIDING BILLIARD BALLS.

LANDON
What the?

CHRISTIAN
Current reaming boulders along the river bed. No trace of the helicopter or the meteorite, by the way.

LANDON
Steve will be overjoyed.

CUT TO:

INT CAVE

Landon awakes to find Christian adding more wood to the fire.

LANDON
I was asleep.

CHRISTIAN
Yes. Best thing. You might like to roll over and dry your clothes on the other side.

LANDON
We'll have to move, come morning.

CHRISTIAN
I'm pleased you see that.

LANDON
Indians camped by cataracts so settlers wouldn't spot camp-fire smoke in the spray, didn't they? Or, was it settlers out to evade Indians?

CHRISTIAN
Little chance of anyone identifying the crash site from the air, even in good weather. Everything drowned or washed away. Besides which, we're in a dark gorge.

LANDON
The pilot?

CHRISTIAN
No sign.

LANDON
Was it Captain Miller? I should know. Someone will have to notify his wife. Did he have a wife? Did he have children?

CHRISTIAN
I haven't a clue.

LANDON
Why is this happening?

CUT TO:

EXT U.S. COUNTRY ROAD
P.O.V. MAN IN SKI MASK
NIGHT

*A car pulls to a stop. Man in Ski Mask hauls a naked **DEAD YOUNG MAN** out of car trunk. The Dead Young Man has been slashed by a knife. The Man in Ski Mask lays the Dead Young Man beside the road and kicks him over the embankment.*

CUT TO:

EXT CAVE
DAY

Landon emerges from the cave.

LANDON
Christian?

Landon wanders down to the river and finds the Pilot's body washed up on the rocks.

EXT CAVE

Christian returns to the cave, finds Landon gone but spots him down by the river. He goes to him.

CHRISTIAN
Here you are. I've scouted our way up top.

Christian spots the Pilot's body.

LANDON
We have to bury him. Can't leave him to the bears.

CUT TO:

EXT U.S. COUNTRY ROAD
DAY

POLICE *recover Dead Young Man, lugging the corpse, already in a body bag, up the slop.* **INSPECTOR DWIGHTON** *watches.* **SERGEANT TOLLER** *approaches Dwighton.*

TOLLER
That's three. Maybe four if we count the partial.

DWIGHTON
Spread the word that I'll have the badge of anyone who leaks this to the press.

CUT TO:

EXT WOODS/STEEP INCLINE
DAY

Landon and Christian are about to exit the gorge into the thick forest up top.

CHRISTIAN
How are you holding up, buddy?

LANDON
Am I?

Landon and Christian make the top.

LANDON
So sorry.

Landon collapses.

EXT WOODS
NIGHT

Landon sleeps in Christian's cradling arms before a fire.

EXT WOODS
DAY

Christian uses a crudely-fashioned travois to pull Landon's unconscious body.

CUT TO:

INT CITY MORGUE

Inspector Dwighton and the **MEDICAL EXAMINER** *stand over the body of the Dead Young Man, knife striations on the body of the naked corpse.*

MEDICAL EXAMINER
    Same as the others. I'd bet money on it being the same sharp instrument, too.

CUT TO:

EXT WOODS
DAY

Landon is unconscious as Christian flags down a rescue helicopter.

CUT TO:

INT BAR

LENNY SLYNT *and* **KEVIN SILNER** *drink beer.*

LENNY
    Isn't the same, is it? Same shabby look. Same dingy lighting. Seemingly the same prostitutes and hustlers and dopers and hangers-on. The same soldiers, only older. But it's not Iraq.

KEVIN
    Still wishing you were back?

LENNY
Anywhere the smack is cheaper. Speaking thereof, it's time for a stroll to the can. Want to come? My treat. I scored before I got here. We'll fly high and tell war stories.

KEVIN
You-know-who would have my ass.

LENNY
Juan knows the score, buddy. His daddy and brother were dopers.

KEVIN
You go ahead.

INT BAR/MEN'S RESTROOM

Lenny, feeling good, exits a toilet stall. Kevin comes in and almost knocks Lenny over.

KEVIN
I need that hit. Bad. Now.

LENNY
What's the matter, Kev? Juan no longer seem such a ball-breaker when the need sets in full-force?

KEVIN
Come on, Lenny. Hand over.

Before Lenny can comply, Kevin pats him down and stops when he comes up with a syringe.

LENNY
Not that one, buddy. Wouldn't want to give you anything besides a good time. Not that I'd check positive. Damn it, Kevin. Cool it.

KEVIN
I need it now. Not tomorrow. Not next week.

LENNY
What's the matter with you? See a ghost?

KEVIN
The ghost saw me, too.

CUT TO:

EXT CITY STREET
NIGHT

Lenny Slynt emerges from an all-night liquor store and heads to his place. A **MAN** *attacks him, but Lenny gets the better hand. He drags the Man into an alley and empties the Man's pockets, finding a wad of bills. There's a military tattoo on the Man's right forearm. Lenny gives the Man a few kicks for good measure and heads off.*

CUT TO:

INT BEDROOM
NIGHT

*Kevin Silner has a nightmare which **JUAN** tries to bring him out of.*

CUT TO:

INT FEASWELL CLINIC/THERAPY ROOM

*Landon enjoys a hot-water pool. **CARL WEST-INGHAM** and Kevin Silner are poolside.*

LANDON
  Days a blur or blank. Christian discharged two days ago.
(to Kevin)
  I'll understand if you want to split.

KEVIN
  I'm fine.

CARL
(to Landon)
  You look surprisingly well after what you've been through. The newspapers are still full of it. Great for business, by the way. Sales are up.

LANDON
  Hardly consolation, I'm so black and blue.

CARL
  Don't rush recovery. I'll hold the fort.

KEVIN
(to Landon)
  I brought you a get-well gift.

Kevin gives Landon a bracelet of filigreed bleached turkey bones.

CARL
   I still can't figure out how he gets such detail in those things.

LANDON
(to Kevin)
   This has to be your best.

CARL
   He insisted he bring it himself, too.
   Kevin in a hospital; Daniel in the lions' den.
(checking his watch)
   We should head on out. Williams is bringing in some new carvings. He asked about you. So did your other artists. Everyone waits to hear if and when you're up to visitors.

LANDON
   I hope to be out of here faster than Dr. Feaswell expects.

Carl and Kevin exit, but Kevin returns.

KEVIN
   I told Carl I left my cigarettes. I had to tell you about "The Spaceman."

LANDON
   Who?

KEVIN
> The ghost. I saw him. Worse, he saw me.

*The door opens. Steve Howard and U.S. Army **MA-JOR SAMPSON** enter. Sampson wears a holstered military revolver.*

STEVE
(to Landon)
> Finally back among the living, are you?

In his anxiousness to exit, Kevin almost knocks over Steve and Sampson.

STEVE
(of Kevin)
> A man in a hurry.
(to Landon)
> Landon Jordan, Major Sampson.
(to Sampson)
> Major Sampson, Landon Jordan.

LANDON
> Your helicopter, was it?

SAMPSON
> Officially the U.S. taxpayers'. I arranged for its use. Liaison.

LANDON
> Steve's use? Candell Technology's use?

SAMPSON
> I always thought Steve was CanTech.

STEVE
Talk like that will make you my friend but will put a few other noses out of joint.

LANDON
There's very little to tell you, Major, or tell the taxpayers. The copter crashed, washed down a river and over a falls. One minute, we were in the sky; the next minute, we were in the water.

STEVE
The Major sent a team to the crash site. The team would have been there sooner if we'd had Christian's full cooperation.

SAMPSON
Dr. Feaswell kept Christian off-limits for three days.

STEVE
Christian unavailable, you comatose, we had no success locating the crash site on our own. You'd covered a surprising distance on foot; the wreckage was in a gully and scattered. Not easily spotted. The weather erratic.

SAMPSON
It was only after Feaswell allowed us access to Christian that we pinpointed the spot.

LANDON
There's still a problem?

STEVE
The delay allowed someone to go in and get my meteorite.

A MAN enters, dressed as a clinic orderly; he removes a MODEL-12 BERETA SUB-MACHINE GUN from beneath his clinic smock. Sampson is faster and gets off the first shot. Death spasms pull the trigger of the Man's automatic weapon and spray the room with random gunfire. Steve and Sampson are shot, the latter in the arm. Landon seeks cover under the water of the pool.

DR. JOHN FEASWELL, *Christian, and* **CLINIC PERSONNEL** *enter the aftermath.*

CHRISTIAN
Landon?

Landon surfaces.

SAMPSON
(to Clinic Personnel)
Take care of Dr. Howard. Now.

CUT TO:

INT FEASWELL CLINIC ROOM

John pulls curtain from inside to reveal the bed in which Landon lies. Christian enters the room.

CHRISTIAN
(to John)
How is he?

JOHN
Amazing, when you consider the sieve made of that room.

CHRISTIAN
Since when do you hire gun-fighters?

JOHN
He wasn't ours. I know all our Vets.

LANDON
Vets?

JOHN
Tattoo, right forearm. Dead giveaway. Service in Iraq.

CHRISTIAN
A grudge against Major Sampson, then, so he tries to blow away everyone in the room?

JOHN
I'm just a medical doctor, old buddy. You want motivations, you need a psychiatrist's opinion. We have one on staff; shall I send him around? Or, will you ask the police who are due shortly? Speaking of the police, I'll prescribe a sedative so Landon won't have to face their questions until morning.

LANDON
I don't have any answers.

JOHN
That won't stop them from asking.

*A **NURSE** appears at the door.*

NURSE
Dr. Feaswell?

John joins the Nurse. The two confer inaudibly.

JOHN
(to Landon and Christian)
Either of you know Steve Howard's next of kin?

LANDON
Tell me he's all right.

JOHN
Afraid not. It's a miracle that you and the Major survived.

LANDON
Jesus. Steve has a sister somewhere. His wife and son died in a car accident years ago.

JOHN
I'll get someone on it and scrounge up that sedative while I'm at it.

John leaves with the Nurse.

CHRISTIAN
This isn't how I planned our reunion.

LANDON
Did I thank you for hauling my ass out of the wilderness on your back?

CHRISTIAN
Your ass was just too fine to leave behind.

CUT TO:

INT FEASWELL CLINIC ROOM
MORNING

The Nurse draws the curtains on the windows of Landon's private room. Landon is in the bed.

LANDON
Could you tell me Major Sampson's room number, please?

NURSE
He's been transferred to the medical facilities at CanTech.

LANDON
He's all right, though?

NURSE
You'll have to ask his doctor.

LANDON
I'll be checking out of here today, too, by the way.

NURSE
Will you now? Well, I'll be checking with Dr. Feaswell on that if you don't mind. In the meantime....

John enters.

JOHN
Did I hear someone say he wants out? You don't trust Carl Westingham to run things? He seemed competent enough at your gallery last night.

LANDON
I've been so long out of touch, you're now dating my gallery manager?

JOHN
An old mentor is retiring, and I wanted something special to give him. He's an avid yachtsman, and Christian assured me there was nothing more fitting than a piece of Landon Jordan scrimshaw. I chose that marvelous old walrus tusk — *The Marimet Rounding Cape Horn.*

LANDON
I hope Carl gave you a discount.

JOHN
He said he'd talk one over with you today.

LANDON
Consider it a done deal.

JOHN
Then, if you genuinely feel up to it, you're out of here today, by way of thank you.

LANDON
No kidding?

JOHN
People mend faster out of hospitals, even out of mine. Manage on your own two feet throughout the morning, and I'll see your discharge papers are at the front desk by this afternoon. After your scheduled interview with Inspector Dwighton, of course.

CUT TO:

INT FEASWELL CLINIC/SOLARIUM
DAY

Landon and Inspector Dwighton sit at a table.

LANDON
I'm sorry I can't be of more help, inspector. It happened so fast and was so unbelievable in the bargain.

DWIGHTON
You ever see the gunman before?

LANDON
Never.

DWIGHTON
You thought he was just another orderly.

LANDON
When he first came in, yes. I only saw him briefly before the shooting started. Do you have any idea who he was? Someone with a grudge against Major Sampson?

DWIGHTON
What makes you say that?

LANDON
Dr. Feaswell mentioned that the gunman had some kind of military tattoo.

DWIGHTON
Probably a really gung-ho Army-type who never adjusted to life after Iraq. Forensics say he snorted coke prior to the hit; that's the probable reason Major Sampson got the better of him. If we can now prove a bone of contention between him and the Major, we'll have our open-and-shut case.

CUT TO:

INT TAXI
AFTERNOON

Landon wears and fingers the bone-filigree bracelet Kevin gave him.

EXT LANDON'S CONDO BUILDING

*Landon exits the cab, pays the **CAB DRIVER**, and heads up the walk. A car pulls up on the street behind him and stops, Carl at the wheel.*

CARL
Landon?

LANDON
You okay? I called the gallery, and Tilton said he opened for you. No answer at your place. You look horrible.

CARL
Can we talk?

Landon gets in the car on the passenger side.

INT CAR

Landon and Carl sit together in the front set.

CARL
I'm sorry. He made me.

LANDON
He? Made you what?

The Man in Ski Mask lurks on the floor of the car, in the back, with a BERETTA M51 PISTOL.

MAN IN SKI MASK
(startling Landon)
Seems I'm better at this than coke-head Clamer.

43

LANDON
Clamer?

MAN IN SKI MASK
The guy gunning for you but who shot everyone but.

LANDON
Gunning for me?

CARL
It has to do with Kevin.

Landon touches the Kevin-made bracelet around his wrist

MAN IN SKI MASK
You want to pass back your cell phone, Landon.

LANDON
I didn't have one at the clinic. Doctor's orders.

Man in Ski Mask comes suddenly up, leans belligerently over the front seat, pokes his gun in Landon's face, and pats down Landon for signs of a cell phone. Apparently convinced there isn't one, he returns to the back with a grunt.

CUT TO:

INT CAR/DESERTED ROAD IN
FORESTED AREA
TWILIGHT

The car stops, and the Man in Ski Mask comes out of his crouch to display his weapon.

MAN IN SKI MASK
G-U-N, gun: Beretta M51 pistol. Manufacturer: Pietro Beretta, Italy. The latter ring any bells? Hint: Model-12 s.m.g.

CARL
(to Landon)
He prefers knives.

LANDON
(to Man in Ski Mask)
My father made knives.

MAN IN SKI MASK
Your father made knife hilts.

LANDON
You knew him, then?

MAN IN SKI MASK
What I know is how it's time for one of you to spill his guts about Kevin, or both of you end up dead.

EXT CAR

Landon, Carl, and the Man in Ski Mask exit the car.

MAN IN SKI MASK
(to Carl)
    Car keys, please.

EXT BURNED-DOWN CABIN
TWILIGHT

CARL
    I'm so sorry about this, Landon.

MAN IN SKI MASK
    To be even sorrier when you see how much easier it is to interrogate two people, as opposed to one. Especially when the two are friends.

INT BURNED-DOWN CABIN

Carl lifts floor-door to the steep stairwell illuminated by automatic lighting. Carl goes first, then Landon, then the Man in Ski Mask.

CUT TO:

INT APARTMENT ROOM
P.O.V.—**LISTENER**

There's the SOUND of A PHONE DIAL TONE, and the LISTENER clicks on taping equipment. There's the SOUND of A PHONE BEING TOUCH-TONE DIALED, A PHONE RINGING ON THE OTHER END OF THE LINE, THE PHONE ON THE OTHER END BEING ANSWERED, and Landon's recorded voice on the answering machine.

LANDON
This is Landon. I'm not here at the moment. Nor can I say for sure just when I'll be back. You can leave a message after the beep, or contact Carl Westingham at the downtown Jordan Gallery.

There's the SOUND of THE ANSWERING MACHINE BEEP. Kevin Silner's voice comes over the line.

KEVIN
Landon. Landon. Landon.

The Listener picks up a telephone and touch-tone dials.

CUT TO:

INT BURNED-DOWN CABIN/
BASEMENT STAIRWELL

Landon, Carl, and the Man in Ski Mask head down. There's the SOUND of A PHONE RINGING from somewhere below. The Man in Ski Mask pushes Landon's shoulder with his gun hand.

MAN IN SKI MASK
Do move your asses, gentlemen. That call may be important.

Landon loses balance, windmills his arms, grabs the Man in Ski Mask's arm, dips, and tosses the Man in Ski Mask over his shoulder. The Man in Ski Mask lands between Landon and Carl. His gun bounces on the stairs, out of reach. Carl crawls over the Man in Ski Mask and up the stairs. The Man in Ski Mask grabs Carl's foot. Landon lends Carl a hand and frees him. Landon and Carl flee up the stairs.

INT BURNED-DOWN CABIN
TWILIGHT

Landon and Carl exit stairwell and drop-shut the floor-door.

EXT BURNED-DOWN CABIN
TWILIGHT

Landon and Carl attempt an escape.

LANDON
    Do we take your car, or…?

CARL
    He has the keys.

Landon and Carl bypass the car for the woods.

EXT WOODS
TWILIGHT

Landon and Carl are on the run. Both stop.

CARL
    Listen.

LANDON
Birds. Bees. Wind in trees. Gasps for breath. Mine? What?

CARL
I don't hear him.

LANDON
We should be so lucky.

Carl's shirt is partially open. Landon sees bloody knife-cut striations on Carl's chest.

LANDON
He did that?

CARL
I told you he likes knives.

LANDON
Sick sonofabitch!

CARL
I'm going to backtrack and see what the bastard is up to. You wait here.

LANDON
Are you crazy?

CUT TO:

EXT WOODS
NIGHT

Landon waits for Carl who has left but now returns.

CARL
　　He came out of his hole, got in my car, and drove away.

LANDON
　　Where would he expect us to call for help?

CARL
　　Has to be the service station up the road.

LANDON
　　How about the phone in the cabin?

CARL
　　Cellular. He took it with him.

LANDON
　　Damn. Other choices?

CARL
　　Miles to walk.

LANDON
　　From some poem, right?

CARL
　　How do you feel?

LANDON
　　Certainly not up to miles.

CUT TO:

EXT DESERTED COUNTRY ROAD
NIGHT

Landon and Carl walk.

LANDON
Any idea why he wants Kevin?

CARL
Would you believe something to do with mes-
sages from Mars? And I mean literally from Mars.
When he cut me, it was "for them". "They" (not the
Devil, mind you) made him do it.

LANDON
You're not really talking little-green men?

CARL
Believe me when I say that he definitely did
give that impression.

LANDON
My guess: drugs. Kevin's still high, more often
than not, yes? You want more close encounters of
the third kind? Kevin came back after you left the
clinic yesterday and insisted he'd seen some kind of
ghostly "spaceman".

CARL
He ever tell you what happened to him in Iraq?
More than just being a P.O.W. for over three years,
I mean, one year spent locked in those pens where

those thousands of turkeys had been machine-gunned by retreating forces with a Sherman-march-to-the-sea mentality.

LANDON
Kevin told you more, did he?

CARL
You haven't guessed yet that he's my brother, have you?

LANDON
Carl Westingham. Kevin Silner. And you wonder why I didn't guess?

CARL
Kevin changed his last name to save our family the embarrassment of his drug problem. After he ran from the last V.A. hospital, it took me five years to track him down. He only recognizes me part of the time. Only since Juan came into his life has he been better.

LANDON
Juan?

CARL
Boyfriend.

LANDON
And here I thought that was you.

CUT TO:

EXT SERVICE STATION/
OUTSIDE PHONE BOOTH
NIGHT

Landon and Carl are in the tree line. **TWO CUS-TOMERS** *get their cars serviced by one* **ATTEN-DANT.**

LANDON
No sign of your car, right?

CARL
Not that I can see.

LANDON
What do you think?

CARL
Maybe our sick friend got out while the getting was good.

LANDON
You stay put. No sense giving him both of us to shoot at. I'll call John Feaswell. I want him to look at your cuts, and he can help us figure out who has jurisdiction in this neck of the boondocks.

CUT TO:

EXT SERVICE STATION/
OUTSIDE PHONE BOOTH
NIGHT

Landon returns to Carl after completing the call.

LANDON
John and Christian are picking us up and calling Inspector Dwighton.

CARL
So why the worried expression?

LANDON
That crazy bastard could have given us a better run for our money. Why didn't he? Why isn't he here? Why didn't he at least disconnect the phone at the station?

CARL
Talk about a killjoy.

CUT TO:

EXT SERVICE STATION/
OUTSIDE PHONE BOOTH
NIGHT

Landon guards the outside door of the men's rest room wherein John doctors Carl's knife wounds. Christian joins Landon.

CHRISTIAN
They through, yet?

LANDON
He's wrapping some kind of bandage.

CHRISTIAN
Anyone who'd carve on someone else should be put away for good.

LANDON
No argument from me.

CHRISTIAN
Earlier, I had a call from Major Sampson.

LANDON
I still have to thank him for saving my life at the clinic.

CHRISTIAN
They've exhumed the pilot and checked the crash site. The helicopter was rigged to go down. One bomb took out the engine. An anti-personnel devise took out the pilot.

LANDON
I don't believe that. Do you? Who? Why? How? What for?

CHRISTIAN
According to Major Sampson, you're looking at the who.

LANDON
Be serious!

CHRISTIAN

His theory, and Steve's before him: I did it for the meteorite.

LANDON

To make a knife, you mean? Please! You didn't have time to plant a bomb, let alone two. I was there.

CHRISTIAN

A small inconsistency the Major has yet to figure. He's convinced John sent men in to find the meteorite at the crash site while I was under medical lock and key.

LANDON

Why would he think that?

CHRISTIAN

John's a friend and owes me.

LANDON

Did John send in a team? Did they get the meteorite?

CHRISTIAN

Yes, to the first. No, to the second. I had to buy one that went down, on some farmer's land, Nova Scotia, 1972.

LANDON

Steve lost his meteorite. You bought one that went down in Nova Scotia in 1972.

CHRISTIAN
Major Sampson is convinced there is no Nova Scotia meteorite, only the one I pilfered from the crash site.

LANDON
I see where he might.

CHRISTIAN
I told him you knew what Steve's meteorite looks like, but he thinks anything you'd say would be colored by our time together.

LANDON
What shit!

CHRISTIAN
Steve hinted at some kind of sexual hanky-panky going on between us as far back as when our father's collaborated.

LANDON
Does Major Sampson know I was fourteen and in France, and that you were studying aquaculture in Japan?

CHRISTIAN
He knows now. I, also, told him that you weren't the only CanTech team member who saw Steve's meteorite and can tell it from the other one. There were pictures taken, too, yes?

The men's rest-room door opens, John and Carl exit.

JOHN
That's all I can do with what I have. There's a good possibility of scarring. Nothing someone who built his clinic on rhinoplasty and tummy-tucks can't fix.

CUT TO:

EXT LANDON'S CONDO BUILDING
NIGHT

The car with Landon, Carl, John, and Christian stops at police barricade. **PATROLMAN ZELMAC** *approaches the car, Sergeant Toller nearby.*

ZELMAC
You folks have to move.

CHRISTIAN
My friend, here, happens to live here.

LANDON
I'm Landon Jordan, officer.

ZELMAC
(to Sergeant Toller)
Seems we have our incoming for Dwighton.

CUT TO:

INT MANAGER'S ROOMS/
LANDON'S CONDO BUILDING

Sergeant Toller ushers in Landon, Carl, John, and Christian. Inspector Dwighton leads them, sans Toller, to a quieter room and shuts the door.

JOHN
We were expecting a more subdued reception.

DWIGHTON
The best laid plans of mice and men.

LANDON
Is there any reason we can't do this in my condo?

DWIGHTON
A very dead Kevin Silner, for one.

CARL
No!

LANDON
(to Dwighton)
My friend, Carl, here, is Kevin's brother.

DWIGHTON
There's no record of family.

LANDON
A long story.

CARL
I've expected this. Drugs. Buying. Selling. Using. Abusing.

DWIGHTON
He told the building manager he was here to "water Landon's plants." He'd done it before.

LANDON
Once. I went to Europe.

DWIGHTON
He left a disjointed message on your answering machine.

CHRISTIAN
He called before he came?

DWIGHTON
Probably to make sure Landon wasn't back from the clinic.

JOHN
Drugs on the premises?

DWIGHTON
Several packets of coke, high-grade. Left behind by a killer who didn't have much choice after the fight Kevin put up. Neighbors called to report the racket. Could I ask you gentleman to identify the body?

JOHN
You need them both?

DWIGHTON
Mr. Westingham is his brother. It'll help if Mr. Jordan gives his impression of anything missing or out of place.

JOHN
I'd prefer Carl somewhere I can better treat his knife wounds.

DWIGHTON
About his knife wounds....

Carl touches his bandaged chest. Dwighton goes to the door and opens it.

DWIGHTON
(through the open door)
Someone call Delaney. I want him here on the double.

CUT TO:

INT LANDON'S CONDO

Dwighton, Carl, and Landon enter.

DWIGHTON
If either of you get queasy, the bathroom has been dusted for prints, so feel free....

A piece of scrimshaw is overturned on the floor. Dwighton picks it up.

DWIGHTON
A fine piece. Worked by you, Mr. Jordan?

LANDON
Yes.

DWIGHTON
There's a particular style and technique for every artist, yes? This wouldn't have to be signed, and anyone would know it was a Landon Jordan.

LANDON
Only someone who knows scrimshaw and scrimshaw artists.

DWIGHTON
But one artist recognizes the work of another by how the picture is scratched, whether it's a ship or a horse, whether it's in blue, black, or multi-colors?

LANDON
Yes.

Dwighton replaces the scrimshaw piece on the floor and leads the way to the bedroom. Kevin is on the floor, supine, under a sheet. Dwighton kneels to pull back the sheet to reveal Kevin's face.

LANDON
Oh, Kevin.

CARL
Yes, that's my brother.

DWIGHTON
I hate to draw this out.

Dwighton moves the sheet to materialize the scrim-shawed ivory handle of the murder weapon. (The knife is one of the three knives the Man in Ski Mask put in the sponge-lined briefcase when he stole the Wynard collection and murdered Kyle Wynard).

CARL
He did it.

DWIGHTON
He?

CARL
That's the same knife he used to cut me.

DWIGHTON
Your kidnapper, you mean? You're sure?

CARL
I could hardly ever forget.

LANDON
Actually, the knife is likewise one of two made by Kyle Wynard and my father of meteorite found on my father's Canadian wilderness property. My father sold the meteorites to Wynard who melted them down to extract their iron content. Both knives are part of the stolen Wynard collection.

DWIGHTON
It's usual to collect one's own works, is it?

LANDON
If you create beauty and have the resources to hold onto it, why not? Kyle Wynard had plenty of money from his shipping interests and kept most of his knives. Which didn't hurt the value of those few that did make it on the market.

DWIGHTON
You think knives beautiful?

LANDON
Many knifes, most of Kyle Wynard's knives, are fine works of art.

DWIGHTON
Deadly works of art.

LANDON
An ashtray as a weapon is still an ashtray.

DWIGHTON
Strange a knife, its blade by the father of the man with whom you crash-landed, hilted by your father, once in possession of the madman who kidnapped you and Mr. Westingham, ends up killing Mr. Westingham's brother in your condo. You're sure about the knife?

LANDON
Easy enough to prove.

Landon goes to the closet and returns with a box.

LANDON
My father's work files.

Landon sifts through the papers in the box.

DWIGHTON
Your father learned scrimshaw from an Eskimo who sailed whalers out of Kodiak, Alaska, yes?

LANDON
From the son of an Eskimo who sailed whalers out of Kodiak. Chuteni Icebear wasn't as fond of the sea as his father was. He preferred the woods. My dad still had his Canadian wilderness property then; Chuteni did odd jobs and sold his scrimshaw.

Landon pulls a PHOTOGRAPH OF THE MURDER WEAPON from the box and hands it to Dwighton.

DWIGHTON
You seem to be right.

CARL
Are you going to need us much longer?

DWIGHTON
Only a moment or two, please.

Dwighton turns on the answering machine.

KEVIN
(from the recording)
Landon. Landon. Landon.

LANDON
He's definitely on drugs.

KEVIN
(from the recording)
Too dangerous to tell Carl. Dangerous to tell you. I wanted to at the clinic, but that army man and that other guy scared the shit out of me. Heart-attack time. Bad vibes. Sweats. Hot flashes. Shakes. Want you to understand. Want someone to understand. Maybe you can figure. Tonight. Six o'clock.

Dwighton turns off the answering machine.

DWIGHTON
Dead by six-fifteen. Do either of you know why he used his last dying breath to say, "Baseman forgot we had the same teacher?"

LANDON
Spaceman.

DWIGHTON
Pardon?

LANDON
Spaceman. He'd seen the ghost of one, or vice-versa—or both.

CARL
On drugs, he'd seen everything from the Jolly Green Giant to the Cabbage That Ate Cleveland.

CUT TO:

INT MANAGER'S ROOMS/LANDON'S CONDO BUILDING

Landon, Carl, and Dwighton rejoin John and Christian.

JOHN
Finally!

*Dwighton spots **OFFICER BEN DELANEY**.*

DWIGHTON
Delaney. Over here. Mr. Westingham has knife wounds I'd like you to catalog. Get a camera and find someplace private for you, Dr. Feaswell and Westingham.

JOHN
Wouldn't this be better accomplished at my clinic?

DWIGHTON
Humor me by saving time and doing it here. There never seems to be enough time.

Carl leaves with Delaney and John. Dwighton hands the photo of the murder weapon to Christian.

CHRISTIAN
A knife by Landon and my fathers.

DWIGHTON
So sure, so fast? Your father had many knives.

CHRISTIAN
Only three from meteorites. This is one.

LANDON
It's, also, the murder weapon.

DWIGHTON
Add carver of Mr. Westingham.

CHRISTIAN
Detective Paolo Sánchez of the Los Angeles Police Department was here a couple of years back to have me identify another meteorite knife from my father's missing collection. It, too, turned up in connection with a murder. Rather, several murders. Of L.A. hustlers. Seems the blade got so firmly embedded in its last victim, it had to be left behind by the killer.

DWIGHTON
That knife from the second meteorite down on Jordan Canadian property?

CHRISTIAN
From one down in Baja, Mexico, in the twenties. The work of Clement Callahan. It was the knife that originally piqued my father's interest in meteorite knives.

LANDON

Seems, there's a killer out there with a fetish for meteorite knives.

DWIGHTON

Spare me whatever the fanciful conjecture that would have the press proclaiming, "E.T. Killer!" Or "Death Weapons from the Moon!" Banner headlines on every supermarket tabloid. Try conducting a police investigation with every U.F.O. fanatic within six thousand miles tumbling out of the woodwork to hang on your every move.
(to Christian)
How many knives in your father's stolen collection, anyway?

CHRISTIAN

One-hundred-sixty.

DWIGHTON

Why scoop up the lot if you only want three?

LANDON

Maybe he didn't want anyone to spot the trees for the forest.

DWIGHTON

A nut case decides to commit murders with knives from meteorites. He steals three of them, among others, from Kyle Wynard. One gets irretrievably embedded in the body of some L.A. hustler. He then loses knife two while killing a violently protesting Kevin Silner. Not to worry, he still has back-up knife three?

CHRISTIAN
Don't forget, if you ever knew, there were meteorite knives in the stolen Jorglu, Freeburg, and Masnier collections; none were ever returned to circulation.

Carl, John, and Officer Delaney rejoin Dwighton, Christian, and Landon.

JOHN
What does this officer mean? "Carl's cuts definitely fit his M.O."?

CARL
Where, in other words, have you seen cuts like mine?

DWIGHTON
This isn't for public consumption, but we've found similar on at least three dead hustlers.

JOHN
Why haven't I read anything about them in the papers?

DWIGHTON
Dead hustlers seldom warrant major news coverage, and we wanted to avoid undue sensationalism. We still want to avoid undue sensationalism.

CARL
He planned to kill us, then?

DWIGHTON
Neither Mr. Jordan nor you fit his M.O.

CHRISTIAN
Kevin Silner didn't fit his M.O., either, and that apparently didn't stop him. What if the killer is prepared to settle, these days, for whatever the situation brings?

DWIGHTON
It's obvious that Kevin Silner died as the result of a drug deal gone sour. Who but a drug dealer would have had the money to blow on the sophisticated equipment that bugged Silner's phone?

LANDON
If Kevin's phone was bugged, that's how our kidnapper knew Kevin was here.

DWIGHTON
And it's why you two can sleep well tonight: the killer got it from the horse's mouth, as did the answering machine, that neither of you knew anything. Crazies usually remain consistent in their choice of victims when given the choice. How great could this killer's compulsion have been to kill you if he let you go?

LANDON
He didn't exactly let us go.

DWIGHTON
What he did was not give chase. He could have put Kevin on a back burner. Easier to track you in

the woods than once you're back among family and friends, spilling your guts. But he didn't.

LANDON
Why aren't I comforted?

CARL
The same reason I'm not.

DWIGHTON
Sleep soundly. My word on it.

LANDON
Sleep where? Here, on my bed? A dead Kevin for company?

JOHN
My clinic owns a condo for V.I.P.'s. You can stay there.

LANDON
(to Dwighton)
If the gun that killed Steve was a Model-12 Beretta sub-machine gun, you'd better get off your butt as regards still thinking anyone had a grudge against Major Sampson.

CUT TO:

INT V.I.P. CONDO

Alone, Landon is on the telephone.

LANDON
Juan, wait! Landon hangs up the phone and leaves the condo.

EXT V.I.P. CONDO BUILDING
NIGHT

Landon exits condo building and walks down the street. **TWO LATIN-AMERICAN MEN** *appear from the bushes and strong-arm Landon into a passing van.*

INT BACK OF VAN

The van stops. The Two Latin-American Men get out and leave Landon. JUAN LOPEZ gets in.

JUAN
Sorry, but we couldn't be sure you weren't followed. I have no wish to see the killer or the police.

LANDON
I understand your reluctance to see the killer.

JUAN
As for the police...let's just say that the paperwork that allows me to stay in this country won't stand up to close scrutiny. I'm leaving the city. Which doesn't mean I don't want Kevin's killer caught.

Juan hands over a folded piece of paper which Landon unfolds.

73

LANDON
(reading)
Lenny Slynt?

JUAN
He was with Kevin the night of the apparition.

LANDON
Man-from-the-moon apparition?

JUAN
Whatever: Kevin shot up a high from which he never came down. Heroin. Not cocaine. Kevin thought cocaine was the equivalent of pabulum and wouldn't have gone to your condo, or anywhere else, to deal it.

CUT TO:

EXT DOWN THE STREET FROM V.I.P. CONDO

NIGHT

*Landon gets out of the van and heads up the block to the condo building. At the door of the condo, he spots the lower half of **CRAIG SOLLEEN** hidden in the shrubbery. Landon fumbles with his keys, and Christian approaches.*

CHRISTIAN
Landon?

LANDON
Someone in the bushes.

Craig steps out.

CRAIG
Evening, Mr. Wynard.

LANDON
(to Christian)
You know him?

CHRISTIAN
Craig Solleen.

CRAIG
Sorry.

CHRISTIAN
John and I figured you and Carl would sleep safer with someone standing watch.

LANDON
I suppose it's the thought that counts.

CHRISTIAN
No one figured you'd be out for a midnight stroll.

Landon goes into the condo building. Christian follows him to the elevator. Craig remains outside.

CHRISTIAN
What were you doing out?

Landon hands him the paper Juan gave him.

CHRISTIAN
(reading)
   Lenny Slynt?

LANDON
   A friend of Kevin. According to Kevin's boyfriend, Lenny may know something.

The elevator arrives.

CHRISTIAN
   I'll have Craig check out our Mr. Slynt.

CUT TO:

INT V.I.P. CONDO
MORNING

*Landon admits Christian who brings groceries. To-
gether, Landon and Christian prepare breakfast.*

LANDON
   Tell me how and when you decided to trap the
man who killed your father, may have killed hustlers in L.A. and here, cut Carl's chest, and murdered Kevin. Don't look at me as if I haven't the
mathematical genius to add one and one and get
two. Your referencing those stolen collections, that
included meteorite knives, was too specific to be
gotten off the top of your attractive head.

CHRISTIAN

I was interviewed by a free-lance writer for an article on the great knives lost over the years. Big-money blades: the Jilan Dagger with the Kerton Emerald in its hilt; the Samslinton Dirk out of that fancy platinum alloy. A couple of knives from my dad's collection.

LANDON

The meteorite knives?

CHRISTIAN

Actually not. A nasty little number, complete with hidden poison compartment, once owned and probably used, by Catherine de Medici, and a rather nondescript blade on John Wilkes Booth the night he shot Lincoln. This writer had the inventories of several stolen collections, a surprising number of meteorite knives among those missing. Either several thieves had a good deal of them, or one thief had gathered up quite a specialized collection.

LANDON

So, you decided to craft a meteorite knife as bait, out to beat Steve and CanTech out of the meteorite down on park property.

CHRISTIAN

Right after my initial epiphany, the Blendale Collection was ripped off in Houston. Included was a Ken Millson-crafted blade of....

LANDON

...meteorite.

CHRISTIAN
Then the cop appeared from L.A., and I'm suddenly out to nab a psychopath.

LANDON
Never once figuring it better to work with the police. Or, are you?

CHRISTIAN
The police had their chance and came up with zilch. They have a murder weapon in L.A.; it got them nowhere. A murder weapon here isn't going to do Dwighton any good, either. He's too worried about "Outer-Space Killer" headlines.

LANDON
You don't find it inconsistent that the killer used a less exotic blade to kill your father?

CHRISTIAN
Dad wasn't due back for hours. I figure the killer merely picked up the first weapon he found handy.

The PHONE RINGS. Landon answers.

LANDON
(to Christian)
It's Craig Solleen.

CUT TO:

EXT STORAGE WAREHOUSE
DAY

Landon and Christian drive up and stop.

CHRISTIAN
Since Craig is so sure Lenny isn't going anywhere soon, I thought you and I could detour here, for a couple minutes. I have to send the Nova Scotia meteorite to the smelter, and Major Sampson is sending over a couple of the men who were with you at the recovery site. I don't want the Major calling foul after the iron extraction begins.

INT STORAGE WAREHOUSE

Landon and Christian walk through the clutter.

LANDON
Should I start unraveling a thread from my shirt, à la Ariadne?

A net falls on Landon and Christian. **TEX DUPRAY**, *19,* **ROGER CANTREL**, *20, and* **SILVO PETRE**, *20, all wearing Halloween masks, follow through in subduing Landon and Christian.*

CUT TO:

INT STORAGE WAREHOUSE

Landon and Christian are tied, blindfolded, and gagged. Inspector Dwighton arrives to untie them.

DWIGHTON
    What treadmill of disaster are you two running on?

LANDON
    How did you find us?

DWIGHTON
    An anonymous call. Your assailants weren't playing for keeps.

LANDON
    What were they playing for?

CHRISTIAN
    Odds are: For possession of the Nova Scotia meteorite, probably at the behest of Major Sampson.

DWIGHTON
    Except the Major's official inspection group is outside, not a meteorite among them.

CUT TO:

INT CAR
DAY

Landon and Christian drive through a derelict part of town.

LANDON
You're convinced Major Sampson is behind the theft of your Nova Scotia meteorite?

CHRISTIAN
There's something suspect in a mentality that sees me putting two bombs on a helicopter, then checking myself in for the ride so I can endanger you, the pilot, and me, for a piece of stone dropped from the sky. I'm paying someone inside CanTech to get me a copy of the report the Major says indicates sabotage.

LANDON
If you ask me, CanTech came up minus a meteorite, and Major Sampson needed you as a scapegoat. Pure and simple.

CHRISTIAN
You certainly have the typical military mind-think down pat.

CUT TO:

EXT DERELICT PART OF TOWN
DAY

Landon and Christian get out of their car. Craig exits his car and joins them.

CHRISTIAN
Lenny Slynt is where?

CRAIG

Across the street in that gutted building and straight down, halfway to hell. Regular little community of dopers who only come out to score or mug little old ladies and gentlemen to get cash to score some more. A regular rabbit warren of vice, where the only light is what you bring in to bring your drugs to meltdown.

LANDON

Any chance of Slynt coming out?

CRAIG

Not any time soon. Seems he hit a real bonanza the other evening when, rumor has it, he rolled a drunk holding substantial winnings from a high-stakes poker game. Slynt bought enough drugs in with him to keep him squirreled in for the duration.

LANDON

No way the police can smoke him out?

CRAIG

No cop goes down there, not even with a SWAT team. It's a series of forts that would have to be taken one at a time. Not ideal siege conditions, as anyone who's fought house-to-house will tell you. Either of you think to bring a gun?

CUT TO:

INT GUTTED BUILDING

Craig and Christian have flashlights and guns; Landon stays close.

CRAIG
This building is condemned, so don't mind bits and pieces falling all around you.

INT STAIRWELL/GUTTED BUILDING

Landon, Christian, and Craig pause on a lower landing.

CRAIG
Now, fun time really begins.
(through cupped hands)
We're coming in, Slynt!

***DUGLAN MCKAY** stands in shadows just inside the nearby door.*

DUGLAN
No need to shout.

CRAIG
Sneak up on me again, I dare you.

DUGLAN
Slynt says take Landon on through and don't make the mistake that this "shooting gallery" requires you shooting your guns. Not that we don't have guns of our own.

CRAIG
(to Landon and Christian)
Just follow my light and watch for dopers sneaking up close enough to catch one or all of us off guard.

LANDON
Maybe this isn't such a good idea.

Duglan pushes Landon into a chute accessed through a hole low in one wall.

INT SUB-BASEMENT OF GUTTED BUILDING

Landon and Duglan exit the chute onto mattresses spread on the floor of a candle-lit room. Candle in hand, Lenny Slynt observes their arrival.

LENNY
Duglan, give Landon a hand.

LANDON
I don't need a hand.

LENNY
Then, move your own ass, because we're not staying here long enough to be dropped in on by your two companions.

Quickly, Lenny goes to a nearby door, Duglan on his heels.

LANDON
Wait!

Landon follows them on through. Lenny shuts and bolts the door behind them. He tosses Duglan a packet of dope.

LENNY
(to Duglan)
Watch the door.

Lenny leads Landon through a maze. He shuts and padlocks another door, then another, behind them. He uses his candle to light several other candles within the room they end up in.

LENNY
Can't be too careful. Someone tried to whack me the other night. Fellow ex-soldier with an Iraqi tattoo and money-bulged pocket. He still has his tattoo.

LANDON
The man who gunned down Steve Howard had an Iraqi tattoo.

LENNY
Small world, but always big enough for someone to die in. Filled to the brim with good and evil. You know that Kevin learned filigree from an Iraqi collaborator interned at that last P.O.W. camp? When the guards found out, they shot the artisan and broke all Kevin's fingers. That guy traveled a long hard road just to get blown away here.

LANDON
Juan said you'd tell me why.

LENNY
The Spaceman: who and why.

LANDON
Little green man?

LENNY
Give me a break. Captain Miller wasn't green or particularly little. Although rumor did have it that he wasn't much of a man. Not in bed, where and when it counted, anyway. Captain Steven "The Spaceman" Miller. You do remember him, don't you? He did a bit of flying for you and CanTech at one time.

LANDON
You don't mean the Captain Miller who piloted our downed helicopter?

LENNY
One and the same: that's what freaked Kevin. Your boyfriend had already announced to the press that Captain Miller was dead and buried. But, The Spaceman was in that bar, that night, a studly little number on each arm. Seeing him really set Kevin off. Somehow the two hustlers only made it worse.

LANDON
You saw Captain Miller in that bar, too?

LENNY

I was shooting up in the can. Kevin came rushing in for a fix he'd turned down not ten minutes before. I would have sweated blood, too, if I'd seen a ghost and the ghost had seen me.

LANDON

I was there when Christian buried Captain Miller. I was conscious at the time and know a dead man when I see one. Captain Miller didn't resurrect without it being the Biblical Second Coming.

LENNY

Kevin knew him real well in Iraq. Captain Miller pulled the strings that got Kevin reassigned from combat to a desk job in Baghdad. Three months later, Kevin was back "in country." Seemed real-weird happy to be back. Said Spaceman Miller was one sick dude.

CUT TO:

INT SUB-BASEMENT/GUTTED BUILDING

Duglan has flashlight and leads Landon through dark corridors. Duglan stops.

DUGLAN

You'll need this.

Duglan hands over the flashlight to Landon.

LANDON

You won't?

DUGLAN
I'm accustomed to the dark. Just take the stairs at the end of this corridor and don't stop climbing until you're back up top.

LANDON
Christian and Craig? Where are they?

DUGLAN
Just unlatch the next door you come to. You might try knocking and announcing yourself, first, because they're not too pleased to be where they are and might not be all that receptive to just anyone. Presently, I'm sure, they're jealously convinced we've made off with you for immoral purposes.

Duglan disappears, and Landon proceeds to the next door; he knocks on the door.

CUT TO:

INT BUILDING/WAREHOUSE DISTRICT
P.O.V.— MAN IN SKI MASK

Three Halloween masks lie on a countertop. Tex duPlay, Roger Cantrel, and Silvo Petre play cards. The Man in Ski Mask shoots Tex duPlay and Roger Cantrel, but leaves Silvo Petre alive.

MAN IN SKI MASK
You stay right where you are!

SILVO
Who are you? What do you want?

CUT TO:

INT CANDWELL TECHNOLOGY
(CANTECH)/RECEPTION

*Landon awaits **JERRY MCLEAN** who arrives.*

JERRY
Major Sampson is looking forward to seeing
you again.

Jerry leads Landon to the elevator.

EXT/INT MAJOR SAMPSON'S CANTECH
OFFICE

*Jerry knocks and remains outside. One arm in a
sling, Major Sampson greets Landon.*

SAMPSON
How very nice to see you, again.

LANDON
I couldn't let another day pass without person-
ally thanking you for your quick action at the clinic.
It saved my life, as I'm sure you very well know.

Major Sampson waves off the compliment.

SAMPSON

Since you're here, I can relay some good news, regarding your friend Mr. Wynard. Seems I was misinformed as to the cause of Captain Miller's death. Not that the chaps, here, who performed the initial investigation, can be faulted all that much. Unless someone is really proficient in bomb-case investigation, this could and easily was mistaken for a bombing incident. Experts, though, since flown in, by way of confirmation and follow-up, insist the damage done was entirely from force of impact.

LANDON

Now if you can just find the stolen Nova Scotia meteorite, you can be wrong again.

SAMPSON

Oh, I still think that Christian planned its theft as a ruse to hide the fact that there is no Nova Scotia meteorite, only the meteorite he pilfered from the crash-site. Did you see it before it clandestinely left the warehouse? I thought not. All moot: CanTech is putting less emphasis on cosmic research now that Steve is no longer at the helm. New head honcho means new prerogatives. So, Wynard can keep whichever meteorite it is. He went through a helluva lot of effort to get it.

INT CANTECH BUILDING

*A **CANTECH MAN** messes with a CanTech elevator computer program.*

INT MAJOR SAMPSON'S CANTECH OFFICE

Landon and Sampson continue their discussion.

LANDON
Do you suppose it would be possible for me to see Captain Miller's body? It is here, isn't it?

SAMPSON
See it? Whatever for?

LANDON
There are rumors he was seen after the crash, alive and well.

SAMPSON
Nonsense.

LANDON
No one knows that better than I do. I attended his original burial. However, my seeing his body could help set some rumor to rest, once and for all.

SAMPSON
Hardly a pretty sight: an autopsied cadaver.

LANDON
I'd only need see his face. Is there family?

SAMPSON
None that we know of.

Sampson picks up the phone.

SAMPSON
(on phone)
Check the present disposition on the remains of Captain Steven Miller. I'll hold.
(to Landon)
Hopefully, this won't take long.
(on phone)
Under whose authorization?

Sampson hangs up the phone.

SAMPSON
Captain Miller's body was cremated this morning by the order of General Robert Kenteth. As a colonel, Bob Kenteth was Miller's C.O. in Iraq.

Landon stands.

SAMPSON
Should I call Jerry to show you out?

LANDON
A right out the door, a left at the second branching hallway; first elevator on the right all of the way to the main floor.

INT CANTECH BUILDING

The CanTech Man finishes his adjustments to the CanTech elevator computer program.

INT MAJOR SAMPSON'S CANTECH OFFICE

Sampson shows Landon to the door.

LANDON
You wouldn't know why Captain Miller was called The Spaceman, would you?

SAMPSON
Was he? Something to do with aspirations to be an astronaut? Some inside joke known only to his peers?

LANDON
Not a close encounter of the third kind?

SAMPSON
E.T.?

LANDON
Another rumor.

SAMPSON
Tell the *National Enquirer* that Miller would have been out of here, ASAP, on a medical discharge if there'd been even a suspicion of such a thing.

INT CANTECH BUILDING

Landon walks to the elevator and waits. He is joined by a U.S. Army **LIEUTENANT.** *A member of* **CANTECH SECURITY** *hurries down the hallway toward the both of them.*

SECURITY
Lieutenant? I need to see some I.D.

An empty elevator car arrives.

SECURITY
(to Landon)
You're free to proceed, sir.

LANDON
I can hold the elevator.

SECURITY
Not necessary, sir. The lieutenant will take the next available car.

Landon steps inside the elevator and pushes the button for the main floor. The descent starts normally but scarily accelerates to a sudden and jarring stop. The door opens on the CanTech Man.

CANTECH MAN
Landon Jordan?

LANDON
Yes.

The CanTech Man produces a micro-dot and hands it to Landon.

CANTECH MAN
Tell Christian that the security is so tight around here lately that this was the only way I could think to get this to him.

The CanTech Man pulls open a hinged panel on the elevator wall to reveal a red emergency telephone.

CANTECH MAN
Tell whoever answers that your elevator has malfunctioned at SB4. Do it now, so no one will suspect you've been off wandering where you shouldn't and give you a strip search.

The CanTech Man hands Landon the phone, steps out of the elevator. The elevator door shuts between them.

CUT TO:

EXT V.I.P. CONDO BUILDING
DAY

Landon unlocks the front door. Christian comes up to join him.

CHRISTIAN
Come with me.

LANDON
Where?

CHRISTIAN
My company plane. Unless you need a piss-stop.

LANDON
I had all of my piss scared out of me by your man at CanTech, who used a runaway elevator as a

means of delivering a micro-dot copy of the investigative report on the downed helicopter.
(Landon hands the micro-dot to Christian.)
All wasted effort, really, in that Major Samson confessed his experts have since changed their minds about there having been any bombs on board.

CHRISTIAN
Things are looking up, then, are they?

CUT TO:

EXT COUNTRY ROAD
DAY

Police are at the dumping site for Silvo Petre's dead body with knife striations on its chest. Sergeant Topper joins Inspector Dwighton and hands over the I.D. found on the body.

DWIGHTON
A student I.D. card.

TOPPER
This victim might not be a hustler.

DWIGHTON
Copy-cat killer?

TOPPER
Either that, or the killer's M.O. is evolving.

DWIGHTON
God help us if that's happening!

CUT TO:

INT CAR
DAY

Landon and Christian are en route to the airport.

CHRISTIAN
There's a *Time* and a *Blade* magazine in the glove compartment. Check the *Time* obituaries on page sixty.

LANDON
Seems to be quite a few.

CHRISTIAN
The one for Charles Tefson IV.

LANDON
(beginning to read)
Prominent restaurateur. *Et cetera. Et cetera.* A deceased friend of yours?

CHRISTIAN
I had the misfortune, yes, to eat at one of his restaurants.

LANDON
By the sounds of it, not much chance, then, for our having a candlelight gourmet meal there. And another obit for him in *Blade*?

CHRISTIAN
Blade: page seventeen.

LANDON
(reading article headline in magazine)
Big-Name Bowie Knives of the Eighteen-Hundreds.

CHRISTIAN
Paragraph fourteen, line three.

LANDON
(reading from the magazine)
Charles Tefson owns a Bill "Bearpaw" Harlen bowie knife unique in that the blade is crafted from metal melted down...."

CHRISTIAN
(interrupting)
...from a meteorite down in the Sierra Madre del Sur in 1866.

LANDON
And, this fits in, how?

CHRISTIAN
The knife in question is being auctioned off, this very afternoon, Lot twelve-fifty-five.

CUT TO:

INT COMPANY JET PLANE

Christian and Landon sit before a screen that has displayed and magnified the contents of the micro-dot for easy reading.

CHRISTIAN
Actually, this seems to contradict the Major by confirming that Captain Steven Miller was killed by one of two bombs on that chopper.

CUT TO:

EXT GROUNDS/TEFSON MANSION
DAY

*Landon and Christian stroll manicured grounds with **OTHER PEOPLE** there for the auction.*

LANDON
This is quite nice.

CHRISTIAN
Reminds me of my family's country estate. Were you ever there?

LANDON
With my father, you mean? No. I was in France during that whole time.

CHRISTIAN
After Dad died, I had the property on the market for awhile. But he loved it so much, I took it off at the first signs of a serious nibble.

LANDON

I remember my father writing me that he was especially impressed by the smithy there. "Looks like it was transported directly from some frontier town. Rustic veneer, but all of all the modern conveniences for a twenty-first-century knife maker." He approved, too, of the separate sound-proofed workroom provided for visiting artisans, although that room is apparently so well-concealed that Dad often had trouble locating the latch to get into it.

CHRISTIAN

Maybe you and I can someday work on a knife project. I, at the forge. You, in that hard-to-access artisan room, scratching something exquisitely scrimshaw.

LANDON

You still plan your own knife if our killer isn't here to pick up this one?

CHRISTIAN

My staff ferreted out this sale. Our hoped-for bidder might not be as well-informed.

LANDON

He's been on top of things until now.

CHRISTIAN

I know a reporter who can assure me plenty of press should I make my own blade—if and when I can get a meteorite that stays in one place long enough for meltdown. That knife, plus the one I hope to pick up here, if our man doesn't show, are bound to be an attractive package. Yes?

LANDON
You have someone planned for hilting your blade?

CHRISTIAN
I was thinking…maybe, you?

LANDON
Damned right you better be thinking that.

Landon and Christian drift with Other People to the mansion room used for the auction.

LANDON
I've not spotted anyone who even vaguely resembles Captain Miller before or after he got busted up in the crash. Have you?

Landon and Christian enter the mansion room being used for the auction. As soon as they sit, there's an explosion. The room fills with billowing yellow smoke. There's accompanying gunfire and grenades. Christian takes Landon's arm and, the more obvious exits blocked by the panicky crowd, heads them for an adjoining smoke-filled room.

CHRISTIAN
There's got to be a window.

JIM SMITH *is a blur in the smoke-filled room with them.*

JIM
One over here, I think.

LANDON
There.

Christian picks up a chair and throws it through the window. Christian and Landon exit through the smoke.

JIM
(from within the smoke behind)
Help, please.

CHRISTIAN
(to Landon)
Wait here.

Christian returns through the billowing smoke. After a few seconds, Landon joins him to help Jim over the sill of the broken window.

LANDON
(to Christian)
He's bleeding.

Christian peels back Jim's bloodied shirt to reveal shrapnel wounds.

CHRISTIAN
He needs a doctor. Maybe I can find one out front.

Christian leaves. Jim's eyes flutter and open.

JIM
Medic. Medic. Medic. Sorry. I was back in Iraq. Yellow camouflage smoke. Tear gas. Automatic-weapons' fire. Grenades. Forty-m.m. M79 hand-held launchers. Nine-m.m. parabellum sub-machine gun.

LANDON
Model 12? Petro Beretta?

JIM
We had the same teacher?

SOUND OF DISTANT SIRENS.

CUT TO:

EXT TEFSON MANSION/PATIO

SERGEANT DARYL POTLEN *interviews Landon and Christian.* **PATROLMAN HOWARD TOOLE** *stands attendance.*

DARYL
Howard, find somebody and check the where-abouts of Lot twelve-fifty-five.

Howard exits.

DARYL
I'm confused. This Lenny....

LANDON
…Slynt.…

DARYL
…is sure Kevin Silner was killed by Captain "The Spaceman" Miller who was already dead in the same crash that almost killed the two of you?

CHRISTIAN
That's the jist of it.

DARYL
Except, *The Friends of Joe Halloy* have already claimed responsibility for all of this.

CHRISTIAN
Friends of the drug kingpin who was picked up for trafficking and perjury? You see this as drug-related?

DARYL
The D.A. was at the auction.

LANDON
Killed?

DARYL
No, but he won't be up and around any time soon. I'll be frank. I find all of this better explained by Halloy's playmates than by a madman shopping for another knife to kill on instruction from little green men from Mars.

CHRISTIAN
This raid had military overtones.

DARYL
There are plenty of vets out there, these days, to be recruited by organized crime.

Howard returns.

HOWARD
Lot twelve-fifty-five, a bowie knife, is missing. So are Lots twelve-forty-three: an emerald ring; twelve-forty-seven: a miniature Russian icon; twelve-forty: a Romanov snuff box.

LANDON
Our man has always been smart enough to muddy his tracks.

HOWARD
Mr. Grendle says this often occurs.

LANDON
Mr. Grendle is frequently in shoot-outs, with smoke bombs and hand grenades, is he?

HOWARD
He handled the Lenox estate when four items were ripped off in a fire.

CUT TO:

INT HOTEL SUITE

Remnants of a candle-lit supper stand deserted on its cart.

INT HOTEL SUITE/BEDROOM

Landon and Christian finish making love.

LANDON
I got my trip with the man of my dreams, fireworks, romantic candle-lit supper, and delicious dessert. Not bad, considering.

The phone RINGS, and Landon answers. The Man in Ski Mask is on the other end.

MAN IN SKI MASK
I would have hated you hurt in the excitement this afternoon.

LANDON
You're responsible for that carnage!

MAN IN SKI MASK
Certainly not *The Friends of Joe Halloy*.

Christian claims the phone.

CHRISTIAN
(on phone)
You won't get away, you sonofabitch!

MAN IN SKI MASK
I've an address where you'll find something of interest when you fly back.

CUT TO:

EXT BUILDING/WAREHOUSE DISTRICT
DAY

Landon and Christian drive up. Craig Solleen pulls in behind them. Everyone gets out.

CRAIG
Last chance to call Inspector Dwighton.

LANDON
Would he come? Tip-off from a dead man and all?

CRAIG
He might.

CHRISTIAN
Maybe, but he's not invited.

CUT TO:

INT BUILDING/WAREHOUSE DISTRICT

Landon and Christian check out one area, Craig another.

LANDON
What?

Christian kneels beside a tarp which he peels partially back.

CHRISTIAN
One Nova Scotia meteorite found.

LANDON
Do you call Major Sampson, or do I? If that was pilfered from the crash site, it changed size and shape between here and there.

CHRISTIAN
How did our friend know it was here, I wonder.

LANDON
How's he manage anything?

Craig joins them.

CHRISTIAN
(to Craig)
We found the meteorite ripped off from the warehouse.

CRAIG
I found two bodies, direct from some slaughter-house.

CUT TO:

EXT BUILDING/WAREHOUSE DISTRICT
DAY

Landon and Christian stand adjacent to police cars. Inspector Dwighton exits the building and comes over.

DWIGHTON
Concerned citizens generally call first.

CHRISTIAN
We wanted to save you the *Tip-Off from Dead Man* headlines. That said, you're the only one we know who legally deals in dead bodies.

LANDON
(to Dwighton)
Any ideas?

DWIGHTON
Tex duPlay and Roger Cantrel. Students in a class Steve Howard taught on Introduction to Cosmo-chemistry at the University. We've been looking for them since Silvo Petre, a member of their study group, turned up knife-sliced and dead.

CHRISTIAN
They made off with my meteorite because they figured it the property of their martyred teacher?

DWIGHTON
I can live with that.

LANDON
Killed, because a madman wants Christian to make him a knife.

CHRISTIAN
The Inspector can't live with something the press might somehow use to make a monkey out of him.

DWIGHTON
(to Landon)
What if someone told your boyfriend, earlier, that three college kids made off with his precious property? Say your boyfriend killed once to get it and wasn't pleased when he was deprived of it a second time. Certainly, he has enough money to buy however many assassins needed to get it back.

LANDON
This meteorite wasn't washed over that waterfall. There are witnesses, and I'm one of them. There are pictures, too, that'll prove it.

Dwighton leaves.

CHRISTIAN
That man is dealing with a ticking time bomb and hasn't the foggiest notion how to disarm it.

CUT TO:

INT HENWELL SMELTER

The Nova Scotia meteorite is prepared for the extraction of its iron. Landon and Christian watch.

CHRISTIAN
They'll crush it, wash it, pass it through separators and magnetically remove non-ferrous gangue.

LANDON
Gangue?

CHRISTIAN
Garbage.

Landon and Christian are joined by **SAM HENWELL**.

SAM
(to Christian)
Telephone call for you in my office. Guy by the name of Ferguson.

LANDON
(to Christian)
Miller's service record?

CHRISTIAN
Maybe.

SAM
Want me to hold off here until you take your call?

CHRISTIAN
Walk Landon through, will you? I'll catch up.

Christian leaves.

SAM
How far did he get?

LANDON
The gangue.

SAM
On to calcination, then.

INT HENWELL SMELTER

Christian joins Landon and Sam.

CHRISTIAN
I've a meeting.
(to Landon)
You want to stick around here?

LANDON
Long?

CHRISTIAN
Merely a matter of my picking up the package and paying for it.

LANDON
I'll stay here, if I'm not in the way. This is actually interesting.

INT HENWELL SMELTER

Christian joins Landon and produces a file folder.

LANDON
That was fast!

CHRISTIAN
Doesn't take long to jump up and down, scream bloody murder, and make an all-around I-want-what-I-paid-for ass of myself.

Christian hands the file folder over to Landon.

LANDON
This isn't it?

CHRISTIAN
We wanted a picture. This is superfluous and sanitized.

LANDON
(scanning the file-folder contents)
Why no picture?

CHRISTIAN
Typical whitewash.

LANDON
(scanning the contents)
He got a Purple Heart for wounds received under *friendly fire*. He was the only one of his unit who came out of it alive, back from a classified mission that was ordered by Colonel Robert Kenteth.

CHRISTIAN
Can't kill the enemy, call on your own side to provide the body count.

LANDON

The same Robert Kenteth—then a colonel, now a general—is the one who ordered Captain Miller's body cremated. Then-Colonel, now-General Kenteth was Miller's commanding officer in Iraq, according to Major Sampson. It's a coincidence that Miller's old C.O. turns up, here and now, to dispose of Miller's remains?

CHRISTIAN

You have a theory?

LANDON

Captain Miller was nuts: brain waves from outer space. Close encounters of the third kind. Heavily into the Iraq drug-and-sex scenes. Why wasn't he given the discharge Major Sampson said would have been forthcoming?

CHRISTIAN

Because he was blackmailing someone to keep his butt covered. Someone who maybe sent a mission somewhere it shouldn't have gone, then fired on its returning members to make sure there'd be no one left to tell the tale. Colonel-then, General-now Robert (Bob) Kenteth?

LANDON

Certainly someone high enough up the military hierarchy when Captain Miller wanted Kevin assigned a desk job in Baghdad.

CHRISTIAN
Not so high, though, that Kevin wasn't back to the shooting war within three months.

LANDON
Back because of faulty connections, though, or because of a sudden death wish? *Happy to be back in country* was how Lenny described him.

CHRISTIAN
A spaced-out blackmailer we know is dead, because we buried him, has a double who looks enough like him for Kevin to have made a fatal mistake. Back to our best bait to draw out whomever this is: one-hand crafted meteorite blade and hilt, coming up.

CUT TO:

INT JORDAN ART GALLERY

Landon is in the back, out of sight. John Feaswell enters.

JOHN
Anybody home?

LANDON
(making his appearance)
Will I do? Apparently not, if that's you're where-is-Carl look.

JOHN
I was in the neighborhood.

LANDON
Another of your mentors retiring? I hope so; there's scrimshaw to be sold if I want to pay my doctor bills.

JOHN
As your doctor, how are you feeling these days?

LANDON
A little dizzy yesterday. All the heat at the smelter. Don't look at me like that. It wasn't down-and-out, merely whoozy.

JOHN
Tomorrow. Eleven o'clock. My office. By cab. I'll give you lunch and drive you home. It's probably nothing, but I don't approve of your frenetic life-style these days: more shootings, more dead bodies, more runs-in with the police.

LANDON
About the scrimshaw you've come for? Or?

JOHN
I thought Carl and I were scheduled for lunch.

LANDON
A little bird told me that you, also, have Carl scheduled for plastic surgery.

JOHN

In this day and age, there's no reason whatsoever why he need continue carrying around reminders of that freak.

LANDON

You're going to do the surgery yourself, I understand?

JOHN

I don't enjoy administration; I'm merely stuck with it, most of the time.

LANDON

That's what comes of having a clinic named after you.

JOHN

When you see Carl, tell him I'll get back to him when I can get our date-night right.

LANDON

Ah, wait a couple of seconds and tell him yourself.

JOHN

He's here?

LANDON

He's been so like a man in love—although don't tell him I said so—that he's been clumsy-klutz all morning. He spilled coffee on his shirt and just went back to his place for a fresh one. Shirt, not coffee.

CUT TO:

INT FEASWELL CLINIC/EXAM ROOM

Landon finishes dressing after an examination. John enters.

JOHN
Clean slate. Must have been the smelter heat, as you so cleverly diagnosed. Ready for lunch? During which, I can tell you just how much I love Carl. And you can tell me just how much Carl loves me, how much you love Christian, and how much Christian loves you.

INT/EXT FEASWELL CLINIC/WALKWAY
DAY

John and Landon continue their conversation.

JOHN
I saw the write-up in this morning's paper. Second-generation Wynard/Jordan knife collaboration: nice press. Enough to draw the attention of anyone with even a passing interest in fancy cutlery. Your impression of the reporter?

LANDON
The handsome and talented Jack Rawlins?

JOHN
He was sweet on Christian in high school. May still be.

LANDON
Christian sweet on him, here and now?

JOHN
Christian sweet on you, here and now.

LANDON
Jack Rawlins, then, is an excellent reporter who did a good story and got us lots of newspaper column space.

JOHN
Normally, a stay in the country would do you a world of good. However, in the country with Christian playing Vulcan at his country-estate forge is liable to be a genuine danger to your health. You had better be in love to be doing what you're planning on doing.

LANDON
Speaking of love, how goes it with you and Carl?

JOHN
It's coming, figuratively and literally.

INT FEASWELL CLINIC/GARAGE

Landon and John approach John's car. The Man in Ski Mask, gun in hand, emerges from the shadows.

LANDON
You!

JOHN
(to Landon)
This the freak?

MAN IN SKI MASK
(to John)
Where would Landon and your frat-brother, Christian, be on their knife project if not for my providing the raw material? The police might eventually have tracked down those misguided college idiots who stole the Nova Scotia meteorite, since cops do have a knack for catching rank amateurs, but how long would that have taken?

LANDON
You killed three innocent students who should still have had their lives ahead of them.

MAN IN SKI MASK
Forget them. They were nothing but an inconvenience. On the other hand, I've a genuine interest in whatever the outcome of any knife-making collaboration between your boyfriend and you. A booby-trap set for me, for sure, but I'm not deterred, believe me. Nor did you expect me to be, did you?

LANDON
At this stage, the knife isn't anything but a lump of iron.

MAN IN SKI MASK
(to John)
I want that knife Landon and Christian are making for me. At the same time, I propose to retrieve

those of my collection that I've inadvertently lost, because of circumstances beyond my control. I certainly never meant to leave them behind, frustrated by a hustler's muscle tissue that refused to yield, and by Kevin's drug-deteriorated body that surprised me with its retention of military-taught skills of self-defense.

LANDON
The police have those knives as evidence. They won't be handing them over to you any time soon.

MAN IN SKI MASK
How about if I threaten to notify the press about every unsolved murder committed by knives made from outer-space metal; the police at their usual wit's end?

LANDON
How many unsolved murders?

MAN IN SKI MASK
It can't surprise you to hear that I have traveled a bit in my time.

JOHN
You really are out of your mind.

MAN IN SKI MASK
(to John)
We'll have plenty of time to discuss it after we take our leave of Landon. In the meantime, do you mind if I call you *John*? Dr. Feaswell is so formal

between two men who've shared the same man. How is Carl, by the way?

LANDON
John, don't!

MAN IN SKI MASK
(to John)
Listen to Landon. Killing you now would only minutely revise my plans. I could manage with Landon as hostage, in your place, someone besides him hilting the new Christian Wynard blade, but I'm counting on Landon teamed with Christian. You as hostage is better.

LANDON
About these friends of yours….

MAN IN SKI MASK
You don't want an introduction, no matter how much you may think you do.

JOHN
You've known them long, have you?

MAN IN SKI MASK
They arrived at a very critical time in my life, and they helped my mother and me deal with my perverted father and his perverted whoring male prostitutes.

LANDON
Your father was gay and having sex with male prostitutes?

122

MAN IN SKI MASK
Was he?

CUT TO:

INT INSPECTOR DWIGHTON'S OFFICE

Dwighton, Landon, and Christian, are in attendance.

DWIGHTON
We're coordinating with the Los Angeles Police Department.

LANDON
They're actually going to hand over the murder weapon from their hustler murders?

DWIGHTON
They're going to work with us on that possibility and on the alternatives. We have until Christian and you complete your new knife before we need make the final decision on which way to go.

LANDON
He's serious about cutting up John and mailing him piecemeal to the press.

CHRISTIAN
(to Dwighton)
You do anything to get John harmed, and I'll see you have headlines that make *Moonstone Murders* look pale by comparison.

CUT TO:

INT WYNARD COUNTRY ESTATE/SMITHY

Landon sits in the "secret" artisans' room of the smithy, at a worktable, and he works on the scrimshaw handle for the knife blade. He switches on an intercom and listens to the SOUND of Christian HAMMERING STEEL for the blade in the next room. Also, in the next room, there's the SOUND of a PHONE RINGING, and Christian quits hammering. Landon switches off the intercom, for a resulting silence, and he gathers up his work, opens the door, and enters the reproduction of a frontier-town blacksmith's shop. He shuts the door behind him, and it becomes another rustic wall in the smithy, no hint of the workspace behind it. Christian hangs up the phone.

LANDON
Unlike artisans before me, I enjoy the noise. I like watching you make the noise. Will my moving in here distract you?

CHRISTIAN
Glad to have you.

Christian helps Landon set up.

CHRISTIAN
The call was the report on Captain Miller's father. He died in a house fire while the kid and his mother were at the movies. He smoked in bed, and

that was called the cause. Whether or not he slept around with paid male prostitutes is going to be harder to find out, at this late date, his wife dead of cancer.

LANDON
He probably didn't. It wasn't Captain Miller who told me about his perverted father, but the killer who told me about his. The two can't be one and the same.

CUT TO:

EXT WYNARD COUNTRY ESTATE/PATIO
DAY

Landon sits and is joined by Christian with manila envelope.

CHRISTIAN
Finally. Ferguson comes through.

LANDON
A good photo of Miller?

CHRISTIAN
It better be.

Christian opens the envelope.

CHRISTIAN
Bingo!

LANDON
Except, it's not Miller.

CHRISTIAN
Same dark hair.

LANDON
You saw him busted up after the crash. I saw him, on and off, for days. This isn't Captain Steven Miller. Your Mr. Ferguson screwed up again.

CHRISTIAN
Maybe not.

CUT TO:

INT WYNARD COUNTRY ESTATE/SMITHY

Landon and Christian attach the finished scrimshaw handle to the finished knife blade. The Man in Ski Mask appears in BUTTON-FRONT SHIRT and BUTTON-FLY JEANS.

MAN IN SKI MASK
Not surprised? Nothing from you, like: "You're early; the exchange is set for this coming Thursday"?

LANDON
To the contrary, Captain Miller, you're right on our schedule. Take off your silly mask; it's no longer necessary. Make yourself comfortable. We know you weren't anywhere near that helicopter when it, the pilot, Christian, and I went down in it.

126

You did, however, plant the explosives, or at least arranged for someone to do it for you.

CHRISTIAN
Got some sucker to stand in for you, didn't you? Someone who owed you from Baghdad, no doubt.

LANDON
Come on, Captain Miller. This is where the villain is confronted and spills his guts.

CHRISTIAN
Kevin dead because he spotted you alive in the bar. Steve dead because the man you hired to kill Landon flubbed. Bodies, bodies, everywhere.

LANDON
We've your picture. Take a look.

The Man in Ski Mask looks at the photograph.

MAN IN SKI MASK
I've cased this place. It's clean.

CHRISTIAN
Of police, you mean? We don't need the police to help us with you, Captain Miller. You're way too adept at manipulating them.

*The Man in Ski Mask peels off his mask and reveals an older version of the **face in the photo** = UN-MASKED MILLER.*

LANDON
Who was the guy who took the fall for you?

UNMASKED MILLER
Ex-Lieutenant Ralph Lester. One-time-Marine-and-chopper-pilot. A loner. No family. Right color hair and general body build. Perfect for the fools at CanTech who didn't know a fake me from the real me.

LANDON
A convenient way for you to drop out? Getting too hot, was it? Too many enemies? Past history in Baghdad catching up? Colonel now-General Kenteth tired of protecting your sorry ass? Too many dead bodies pointing their fingers in your direction? Your otherworldly advisers telling you what to do and how to do it?

UNMASKED MILLER
My otherworldly advisers, as you call them, were upset that the two of you ended up on that chopper, especially Wynard who was to make them a new blade. Their intervention was what got you both out alive.

LANDON
Fortitude, luck, and leg-power got us out alive.

CHRISTIAN
So protective of knife-makers, are they, that they told you to kill my father who was one of the best?

UNMASKED MILLER
Hardly. They were chagrined as hell when he came home unexpectedly.

CHRISTIAN
They approve of you killing us now, though?

UNMASKED MILLER
They understand the necessity, yes, just as they understood, finally, the necessity of my having had to kill your father.

LANDON
Will it be a necessity to kill John after he gives you a new face?

CHRISTIAN
Surprised we figured that out, are you?

LANDON
You never had any intention of trading John for knives, did you? Always had every intention of letting us try to arrange a little trap to catch you. Always thinking you'd sneak on in early—and here you are—to collect this new knife and, after your new identity given you by John's plastic surgery, leave behind the other knives by way of acceptable sacrifice.

CHRISTIAN
You need a new face, because the substitute dead in your place, on the copter, didn't quite do the job. Then, there's General Kenteth. He knows you're alive. Got you the job at CanTech. Had the

substitute cremated to cover your butt. Thinks you're turning over a new leaf. Figures you're finally out of his life. What does he do when you kill again? And you will kill again, won't you? You'll kill, and General Kenteth will hear about it, calculate your increasing chances of getting caught. And will he want you to implicate him? No way will he want you alive, and he has friends who have spent their whole life-times in training to eliminate the general's enemies. Except, how do they find you with a new face known only to you and to the plastic surgeon you murder after your surgery?

LANDON
There's, also, the man you used to plant the bombs on the helicopter, plus the men recruited for storming the auction, and the man who monitored the phone calls to and from Kevin's apartment. A new face hides you from one and all.

CHRISTIAN
Good job of pulling your photos, but we found a stray one. How many more out there that you failed to get? Do you risk someone, somewhere, sometime, finding another and saying, "That's not the guy who went down on that CanTech chopper!"?

LANDON
Where's John?

UNMASKED MILLER
Forget John. Where's Mr. Westingham? And don't pretend that he's not on the premises, because I saw him arrive.

In the secret artisan room, Carl, who watches through a peephole, and listens through an intercom, pushes out on the door which strikes Unmasked Miller and knocks the gun out of his hand. A scuffle ensues. Landon, Christian, and Carl are victorious.

INT WYNARD COUNTRY ESTATE/SMITHY

The Unmasked Miller is strapped supine to a workbench. Alone with him, Carl fondles the finished meteorite-blade knife.

UNMASKED MILLER
I'm not going to tell you where your pervert lover is.

CARL
We've yet to see what you will and won't tell me.

UNMASKED MILLER
Idiot sodomist. Male whore. Male slut.

CARL
I'm wondering if your otherworldly friends are even now trying to persuade you to use John as a bargaining chip to save your sorry ass. Yes? No?

UNMASKED MILLER
Me to know.

CARL

Listen to them very carefully if they are, because you need every bit of advice they're willing to give you.

UNMASKED MILLER

Maybe I'll tell the police where John is. Maybe I won't.

CARL

The police have never done a good job handling you. We can't count on them to start now.

Carl emphasizes his possession of the knife by brandishing it.

CARL

I do wonder—don't you—if I'll prove as expert as you in carving human flesh, especially without butchering instructions from on-high?

UNMASKED MILLER

I talk only to the police.

CARL

I'm very fond of John. I want him back even more than the police want him back. And, you're going to perform the magic for me of bringing him back.

UNMASKED MILLER

You're forgetting my friends.

CARL

Am I? Where are they? What do they tell you? Are they really pleased with the failure you've become? You are caught. You are soon to pay the consequences of being caught. No time soon will you again be cutting up or sacrificing anyone else. Making you, at least in my humble opinion, somewhat useless as far as they're concerned. What do you think?

UNMASKED MILLER

They won't desert me. I've served them too well.

CARL

What say we compare how well they serve you in comparison to how well you serve this wants-his-lover-back knife-wielding queer?

UNMASKED MILLER

You'll end up in jail for life, even if I do tell you.

CARL

Charged with what? You seem to forget that you've already been declared legally dead before I even start on you.

With the knife, Carl cuts off the Unmasked Miller's shirt buttons, one at a time, from top to bottom. He cuts off the top button of Carl's jeans' fly.

FADE OUT TO BLACK.

MOONSTONE MURDERS, BY WILLIAM MALTESE

Unmasked Miller lets out a blood-curdling scream.

ROLL FINAL CREDITS.

ABOUT THE AUTHOR

WILLIAM MALTESE was born in the Pacific Northwest. He has a B.A. in Marketing/Advertising and spent an honorable tour of duty in the U.S. Army, achieving the rank of E-5.

He started his authorial career writing for the men's pulp magazines and has since penned more than 150 books, both fiction and nonfiction. According to queerhorror.com, this included the first gay werewolf novel ever published. He also has written a number of bestselling women's romances under the name "Willa Lambert" for houses such as Harlequin and Carousel, including the internationally acclaimed Harlequin SuperRomance #2 (*Love's Emerald Flame*), which is being reprinted by the Borgo Press imprint of Wildside Press along with many of his other novels.

He encourages his fans to visit his websites:

www.williammaltese.com
www.myspace.com/williammaltese